THE CHRISTIAN
MOTHER GOOSE
TREASURY

Library of Congress Catalog Number: 80-69167
ISBN 0-933724-01- 2

Printed in the United States of America.

First Edition Oct. 1980
Second Edition Dec. 1980

THIS BOOK
IS GIVEN AS A
HAPPY FRIEND

To.............................

From...........................

THE **CHRISTIAN MOTHER GOOSE** TREASURY

Paraphrased Text and Original Text
by
Marjorie Ainsborough Decker

Illustrated by
Glenna Fae Hammond
Marjorie Ainsborough Decker

C.M.G. Productions, Inc.
Grand Junction, Co. 81501

Distributed by: Fleming H. Revell Company, Old Tappan, N.J. 07675

TO
MY HUSBAND DALE
WHOSE
LOVE AND ENCOURAGEMENT
NURTURED THIS VOLUME
TO FRUITION
AND
WHO SHARES WITH ME
THE HOPE
THAT
THIS BOOK WILL BLESS
ALL CHILDREN EVERYWHERE

STORYTELLER'S NOTE

". . . Where your treasure is, there will your heart be also."

The warm reception to the original CHRISTIAN MOTHER GOOSE BOOK was so overwhelming that it swept a tide of renewed vigor into the task and vision to complete THE CHRISTIAN MOTHER GOOSE TREASURY. Letters from unexpected places all across the world have been a source of joy and inspiration to see Mother Goose with the message of God's love in Christ, ". . . leap over a wall."

"Once upon a time . . ." is still the phrase that for centuries has been the gateway of expectancy to all the wonder that lies beyond those simple words. Once upon a time God sent forth His Son to reveal to us the greatest story ever told—"God so loved the world, that He gave His only begotten Son, that whosoever believeth in Him should not perish, but have everlasting life."

Why do I use Mother Goose to convey eternal truths? As everyone knows, she is a nostalgic story-teller in the hearth and home of generations past and present. And under her ballooning skirts, the impossible becomes perfectly possible. Yet it takes even greater imagination to envision a river parting, or a man walking on water. But they did! Indeed, imagination and truth are not mutually exclusive. For what is faith without imagination? Who can see eternal life? But those of faith have seen it! Delightful evidences of God's great imagination are all around us— a pelican's pouch, a praying mantis, a melon that houses more than 380 seeds (I counted them!), even you and I!

Some of these observations took root in my mind as a little girl of seven in Liverpool, England. Stories, tales, and parables were part of my childhood. To the sincere question of what is a parable, I was told: "A parable is an earthly story with a heavenly meaning." I pondered this for years as I looked at the parables the Lord Jesus told. Why did the Master of all words choose to tell stories of this kind to stir the hearts of His listeners to search for truth?

There is the graphic parable of the sower who went forth to sow seed. Mother Goose, as a legendary story-teller, has sown seeds into the hearts of children everywhere.

In *The Christian Mother Goose Series*, she now sows the seed of the eternal truths of God's Word. I trust the seeds and parables found in THE TREASURY will help to build a bridge between these earthly stories and their heavenly meanings, and bring a child eagerly yet gently across that bridge into the security and love of God.

Someday the storybook tale behind *The Christian Mother Goose Series* may be told, with all of its "Nothing-Impossible-Possum" adventures. In the meantime, THE CHRISTIAN MOTHER GOOSE TREASURY is sent forth with my prayers and hope that the young and the young-at-heart will search out the hidden treasures in this book, and be led into God's loving fellowship.

With the completion of THE TREASURY, I commit it to His blessing, as I look forward to the rewarding task of completing the third and final volume of THE CHRISTIAN MOTHER GOOSE TRILOGY.

Marjorie Ainsborough Decker

OLD MOTHER HUBBARD

Old Mother Hubbard
   Went to the cupboard,
To get her poor dog a bone;
   But when she got there
The cupboard was bare,
   And so the poor dog had none.

She went down the street
   Her good neighbors to meet,
And they all gathered round her in prayer;
   And when she got back,
She found bones in a sack
   Saying, "God wants us all to share!"

DING, DONG, BELL

Ding, dong, bell,
   There's gladness in the well!
Who put it in?
   God! It's genuine!
Who can get it out?
   Anyone who doesn't doubt.
Ding, dong, bell,
   There's gladness in the well!

7

LITTLE ROBIN REDBREAST

Little Robin Redbreast
　　Sat upon a rail,
Niddle-naddle went his head,
　　Wiggle-waggle went his tail.

Little Robin Redbreast
　　Sang upon a rail,
"Thank You, Lord," went his head,
　　"Praise You!" went his tail!

ONCE I SAW A LITTLE WORD

Once I saw a little word
　　Come hop, hop, hop;
It wasn't kind at all,
　　And I cried, "Stop, stop, stop!"

Once I saw a little word
　　As soft as heather;
I blew it through my lips
　　And said, "Go on forever!"

BOW, WOW, WOW

Bow, wow, wow,
  Whose dog art thou?
Little Tom Tinker's dog,
  Bow, wow, wow.

Bow, wow, wow,
  Who madest thou?
Little Tom Tinker's God!
  Bow, wow, wow.

GO TO BED LATE

Go to bed late,
  Stay very small;
Go to bed early,
  Grow very tall.

Seek the Lord late,
  Treasures are small;
Seek the Lord early,
  Treasures are tall.

ROCK-A-BYE, BABY

Rock-a-bye, baby,
  On the tree top,
When the wind blows
  The cradle will rock;
Mother will make
  The baby a shawl;
God will keep baby,
  Cradle and all.

HICKETY, PICKETY,
MY BLACK HEN

Hickety, pickety, my black hen,
She lays eggs with quill and pen;
Gentlemen come every day
To see what my black hen's eggs say.

Some say, "Ask,"
Some say, "Given,"
Some say, "Come — and be not driven."
Some say, "Seek,"
Some say, "Find,"
Some say, "Leaving things behind."
Some say, "Coming back again,"
Hickety, pickety, my black hen.

11

DOCTOR FOSTER

Doctor Foster went to Gloucester
In a shower of rain;
He went to teach,
He went to preach
God's Word, and make it plain.

LITTLE NANCY ETTICOAT

Little Nancy Etticoat
  In a white petticoat,
With a little light
  That glows and glows!
Never tries to hide it;
  All the town has spied it!
Little Nancy Etticoat's
  Little light grows!

A DILLAR, A DOLLAR

A dillar, a dollar,
  A ten o'clock scholar,
He's on time for his church school!
  He got up early in the morning
To keep the Golden Rule:
  "Love the Lord
  With all your heart,
  And all your playmates, too!"
A dillar, a dollar,
  A ten o'clock scholar,
God is watching over you!

13

TEN LITTLE MISSIONARIES

GO YE INTO ALL THE WORLD WITH
GOOD NEWS! GOOD NEWS!

Ten little missionaries,
  Holding up a sign;
One went to Zanzibar,
  Then there were nine!

Nine little missionaries
  Learning to translate;
One went to Washington,
  Then there were eight!

Eight little missionaries
   Looking up to Heaven;
One went to the Isle of Man,
   Then there were seven!

Seven little missionaries,
   Building with red bricks;
One became a farmer,
   Then there were six!

Six little missionaries,
   To the woods arrive;
One went back home again,
   Then there were five!

Five little missionaries,
   On a lake shore;
One went to mend a net,
   Then there were four!

Four little missionaries,
  Singing happily;
One went to tell Good News,
  Then there were three!

Three little missionaries,
  Praying what to do;
One went to his friend's house,
  Then there were two!

Two little missionaries,
  Sailing to Ceylon;
One got off at Egypt,
  Then there was one!

One little missionary,
  Praising God's dear Son;
Flew into the clouds,
  And then there were none!

RUB-A-DUB-DUB

Rub-a-dub-dub,
　Three boys in a tub,
Getting as clean as can be.
　Rubbing and scrubbing,
And scrubbing and rubbing,
　To please their mommy, you see.

THE ANT

I would not crush
　A little ant
That hurries through the grass,
　For God spent time
To make him;
　So I shall let him pass.

19

PUSSY-CAT, PUSSY-CAT

Pussy-cat, Pussy-cat,
  Where have you been?
I've been to Sheba
  To see the Queen.
Pussy-cat, Pussy-cat,
  What did you there?
I crept in to listen
  Under her chair.

Pussy-cat, Pussy-cat,
  What did she say?
She said she had traveled
  A long, long way.
Pussy-cat, Pussy-cat,
  Where did she go?
To Solomon's land
  With gifts to bestow.

Pussy-cat, Pussy-cat,
  What did she see?
A great, famous King,
  Wise and glorious was he.
Pussy-cat, Pussy-cat,
  Is her tale bold?
No! She said that the half
  Has not yet been told!

20

AS I WAS GOING TO ST. IVES

As I was going to St. Ives,

I met a man with seven cows.

Each cow was strong and fat,

But seven thin cows came after that.

Then came seven fat ears of corn,

Next came seven ears, thin and worn.

  Cows - thin! Cows - fat!

  Ears - thin! Ears - fat!

Who was the man who dreamed all that?

I THANK YOU, LORD

I thank you, Lord,
I thank you twice,
For all your love,
For all that's nice;
I thank you, Lord,
I thank you thrice,
For Jesus' love
And sacrifice.
I thank you, Lord,
Times five, six, seven,
For making me a home in Heaven.

THE MAN IN THE WILDERNESS

The man in the wilderness
　　Said to me,
"How many children
　　Walked through the Red Sea?"
I answered him
　　As I thought I should,
"As many as God said there would!"

A ROBIN AND A ROBIN'S SON

A robin and a robin's son,
  Once went to town to buy a bun.
They couldn't decide
  On plum or plain,
And so they went back home again.

Then robin and the robin's son,
  Decided to agree on plum.
So back to town
  They went once more,
And wished they had agreed before!

WATCH!

Watch the little silkworms spin;
   Watch the squirrels gathering in
Nuts for winter's food to share,
   Telling friends, "Prepare! Prepare!"

Watch the dormouse make a bed;
   Watch the spider spin his thread,
Weaving webs with utmost care,
   Telling friends, "Prepare! Prepare!"

Watch the ants go scurrying by;
  Watch the bees as on they fly,
Gathering pollen here and there,
  Telling friends, "Prepare! Prepare!"

"Watch!" The Lord says, "watch the sky!
  Watch for Jesus' trumpet cry."
Boys and girls from everywhere,
  Telling friends, "Prepare! Prepare!"

BETTY BOTTER

Betty Botter did but mutter,
  "But," she said, " the mutter's bitter;
If I'm bitter while I mutter,
  It will fill my heart with clutter;
But a bit of better chatter,
  That would make my heart feel better."
So she sought some words to fit her,
  Which were kind instead of bitter;
Soon she sang and didn't mutter,
  So kept out that awful clutter;
So 'twas better Betty Botter
  Changed from bitter things to better!

DIDDLE, DIDDLE, DUMPLING

Diddle, diddle, dumpling,
  My son John,
Prayed in bed
  With his stockings on;
The angels laughed,
  And peeped, one by one,
To see John praying
  With his stockings on.

Diddle, diddle, dumpling,
  My son John,
Sang and praised
  With no stockings on!
Ten little toes
  Praising God's dear Son;
Diddle, diddle, dumpling,
  My son John.

27

THE MUFFIN MAN

Do you know the Muffin Man,
  The Muffin Man,
  The Muffin Man?
Do you know the Muffin Man
Who lives on One Way Lane?

Yes, I know the Muffin Man,
  The Muffin Man,
  The Muffin Man,
Yes, I know the Muffin Man
Who lives on One Way Lane.

ONE WAY
LANE

Did you taste the Manna Bread,
  The Manna Bread,
  The Manna Bread?
Did you taste the Manna Bread
He gives on One Way Lane?

Yes, I tasted the Manna Bread,
  The Manna Bread,
  The Manna Bread,
Yes, I tasted the Manna Bread
He gives on One Way Lane.

Will you walk with the Muffin Man,
  The Muffin Man,
  The Muffin Man?
Will you walk with the Muffin Man
Each day on One Way Lane?

Yes, I'll walk with the Muffin Man,
  The Muffin Man,
  The Muffin Man,
Yes, I'll walk with the Muffin Man
Each day on One Way Lane.

THERE WAS A MAN
WHO SOWED SOME SEED

There was a man
  Who sowed some seed,
And some fell by the road;
  The birds flew down,
And ate the seed
  The moment that he sowed.

Some seed fell down
  Upon the rocks;
The soil was very thin;
  And when the sun
Shone very hot,
  They shriveled up within!

Some seed fell down
   Among the weeds,
But couldn't find much room
   To sprout a root;
They were so pressed
   There wasn't room to bloom!

Some seed fell down
   Upon good ground;
They grew and grew and grew!
   Thirty, sixty —
A hundred flowers
   Burst from that tiny few!

PETER WHITE

Peter White will ne'er go right,
Would you know the reason why?
He follows his nose
Wherever he goes,
And that stands all awry!

Now Peter White has solved his plight,
And learned to navigate;
No matter his nose,
He looks where he goes
To God's Word to keep him straight!

WHEN I LOOK UP AT A STAR

When I look up at a star,
  I know it's very, very far.
When I look up at the sky,
  I know it's very, very high.

When I try to find the sea,
  I know it's very far from me.
When I see a mountain tall,
  I know I'm very, very small.

But when I look to God on high,
  Who lives beyond the starry sky,
I know that He will always be
  Very, very close to me.

MOLLY, MY SISTER, AND I

Molly, my sister,
　　And I fell out,
And what do you think
　　It was all about?
Her skirt was long,
　　Mine came to the knee;
And that was the reason
　　We couldn't agree!

Molly, my sister,
　　And I fell out,
But what do you think
　　Turned us round about?
I loved her,
　　And she loved me;
And that was the reason
　　We could agree!

BLOW, WIND, BLOW

Blow, wind, blow!
 Go, mill, go!
Go by the four winds together;
 Breathe on the valley
That's very dry,
 Bring in the corn
And the wheat and rye.
 Blow, wind, blow!
Go, mill, go!
 Go by the four winds together.

HOW MANY MILES TO BETHLEHEM?

How many miles to Bethlehem?
   Three score miles and ten.
Can I get there by candlelight?
   Yes, and back again.

How many miles to Heaven?
   More than three score and ten.
Can I get there by Daystar-light?
   Yes, and back again!

OLD KING COLE

Old King Cole
Was a merry old soul,
And a merry old soul was he;
He called for the Lord
To save his soul,
And he called for his fiddlers three.

Every fiddler
Had a fine fiddle,
And a fine fiddle ministry;
Oh, for song and prayer
None can compare
With King Cole and his fiddlers three!

JEREMIAH OBADIAH

Jeremiah Obadiah
  Climbed the wall of Nehemiah.
With a trumpet in his hand,
  He woke the folk across the land.

BYE, BABY BUNTING

Bye, baby bunting,
  Mother's gone a-hunting,
To get a bulrush basket skin
  To hide the baby bunting in.

DAFFY-DOWN-DILLY

Daffy-Down-Dilly
Has come to town,
In a yellow petticoat
And a green gown.

"Did you work very hard
   To spin cloth by the yard?"
Said a blue-bird to Daffy-Down-Dilly.

"I must really confess
   It's a dazzling dress,"
Said a frog from a pink water-lily.

"How much dye did it take,
   Such bright yellow to make?"
Said a honeybee in the blue heather.

"Tell me, how did you grow?
   Then your secret I'll know,"
Said the wise owl with pen of brown feather.

"No! I did not work hard
To spin cloth by the yard;
And I did not buy dye for this yellow.
As to how I did grow...
Please consider this, so
You can learn of my secret, good fellow:

Where God placed me
    I grew!
In the spot
    Where He knew
Was the best
    For a Daffy-Down-Dilly.
So I stayed
    Rooted there,
And with His
    Loving care
I bloomed into
    A beautiful lily!"

"Consider that, now!"
  Said the wise old owl;
"I must write it down
  With my brown feather."
"Consider that, now!"
  Said the bird, frog and bee,
And they all considered together,
     HOW...
Daffy-Down-Dilly
  Had come to town,
    In a yellow petticoat
    And a green gown!

43

HERE WE GO ROUND THE MIRACLE BUSH

Here we go round the miracle bush,
  The miracle bush, the miracle bush;
Here we go round the miracle bush,
  We go around like Moses.

Take off our shoes, it's holy ground,
  Holy ground, it's holy ground;
Take off our shoes, it's holy ground,
  Take off our shoes like Moses.

Obey the Lord as Moses did,
  Moses did, as Moses did;
Obey the Lord as Moses did,
  Obey the Lord like Moses.

MRS. SPARROW'S
STOLEN EGG

Mrs. Sammy Sparrow
  Had just laid two dotted eggs,
In a nest inside a steeple,
  And off she ran on little legs.

She ran to tell Mrs. Robin,
  "My eggs are marked with an 'E'!
The dots are all arranged that way,
  Would you like to come and see?"

"Yes, I would love to see them,
  What unusual eggs they must be;
But would you take a moment
  For a fresh red raspberry?"

Then while those two dear ladies
    Shared a breakfast raspberry,
Mrs. Blackbird flew on by,
    And those two little eggs did see.

She was quite unhappy,
    Because, that very day,
Her own two eggs had broken
    As she laid them both away.

Now here before her eyes
    Were two eggs, and Mother gone!
"Mrs. Sparrow shouldn't care
    If I steal away just one!"

Then quickly Mrs. Blackbird
 Stole one egg, and off she flew,
Just as Mrs. Sparrow
 And Mrs. Robin came back, too.

"Oh, dear! One egg is missing!"
 Mrs. Sparrow cried loudly.
"Please, Mrs. Robin, watch this egg,
 While I fly to Dandelion Sea."

"Sammy is down there helping
 Grandpa Mole to gather wood;
They won't believe what's happened
 In our happy neighborhood."

47

She flew to Grandpa Mole's house,
  And her tears they dripped and fell,
As she told her sad, sad story;
  And then Sammy cried as well.

"I think that I can solve this,"
  Grandpa Mole said. "Here's a plan;
As Judge of Dandelion Sea,
  I will judge the best I can."

"You say when you came home,
  Mrs. Blackbird flew away?
Then let us go and talk with her,
  And for wisdom let us pray."

GRANDPA
MOLE

So Sammy walked with Mrs. Sparrow;
Grandpa Mole wore his judge's hat;
And all three walked together
To Mrs. Blackbird's for a chat.

"Good-day to you, Mrs. Blackbird."
"It's not a good day," she replied.
"Today my two eggs were broken,
And I cried, and cried, and cried."

"What is that you're sitting on?
It looks like an egg to me,"
Grandpa Mole said slowly;
"Did you have two eggs or three?"

"Oh, I forgot this dotted one,
Your pardon I must beg."
But peeping out was the dotted 'E';
Mrs. Sparrow cried, "That's my egg!"

49

"No! No! this egg is my egg,
  Mrs. Sparrow; you're quite wrong."
"I'm not! The 'E' that marks that egg
  Tells me where it belongs."

Then Grandpa Mole coughed loudly,
  And said, "Ladies, listen to me.
I will decide this matter,
  As Judge of Dandelion Sea."

"We'll share the egg between you,
  By cutting it in two;
Mrs. Sparrow, you take half;
  Mrs. Blackbird, take half, too."

"Oh, no, please do not cut the egg,
    Let Mrs. Blackbird keep it here,"
Mrs. Sparrow quickly said,
    While swallowing a tear.

"I think we should divide it;
    I don't care if it's cut in two,"
Mrs. Blackbird shouted back;
    'Twas then Grandpa Mole really knew —

The real bird mother cared,
    Because she loved her egg, so dear,
And didn't want it hurt at all —
    So Grandpa Mole spoke loud and clear:

"As Judge of Dandelion Sea,
    I hereby now make this decree:
That Mrs. Sparrow is rightfully
    The mother of this egg marked 'E'."

51

Mrs. Blackbird rushed away
    With ruffled feather-clothes,
But Mrs. Sparrow saw a tear
    Roll down her neighbor's nose.

Mrs. Sparrow's little heart
    Felt sad, and so said she,
"I don't think Mrs. Blackbird
    Meant those things she said to me."

Grandpa Mole took off his hat
    And said, "I do agree,
But how to win your friend back
    Takes a special remedy."

"It is written we should be kind,
  And quick to love one another;
Be tenderhearted and forgive
  When we hurt each other."

"It's the best and only way
  To win a hurting friend;
And here's a good suggestion
  To bring about a happy end:"

"There are two orphaned sparrows
  Who need a home and care;
And Mrs. Blackbird's house and heart
  Need someone, too, to share."

"Grandpa Mole, how wise you are!
  Let's go there right away,
To tell our friend, Mrs. Blackbird,
  This is going to be a GOOD DAY!"

PEAS POTTAGE HOT

Peas pottage hot,
  Peas pottage cold,
Peas pottage in the pot;
  Jacob told!
Esau liked it hot,
  Esau liked it cold,
Esau liked it in the pot;
  Esau sold!

DICKORY, DICKORY, DARE

Dickory, dickory, dare,
  A stone flew up in the air;
The giant in brown
  Came tumbling down,
Dickory, dickory, dare.

PETER POSTLE

Peter Postle picked a pack
  Of praising prophets;
A pack of praising prophets
  Peter Postle picked;
If Peter Postle picked a pack
  Of praising prophets,
Where's the pack of praising prophets
  Peter Postle picked?

LONDON BRIDGE IS FALLING DOWN

London Bridge is falling down,
  Falling down, falling down,
London Bridge is falling down,
  My fair lady.

Build it up with wood and clay,
  Wood and clay, wood and clay,
Build it up with wood and clay,
  My fair lady.

Wood and clay will wash away,
  Wash away, wash away,
Wood and clay will wash away,
  My fair lady.

Build it up with iron and steel,
  Iron and steel, iron and steel,
Build it up with iron and steel,
  My fair lady.

Iron and steel will bend and bow,
  Bend and bow, bend and bow,
Iron and steel will bend and bow,
  My fair lady.

Build it up with silver and gold,
  Silver and gold, silver and gold,
Build it up with silver and gold,
  My fair lady.

Silver and gold will steal away,
  Steal away, steal away,
Silver and gold will steal away,
  My fair lady.

What will build up London Bridge,
London Bridge, London Bridge?
What will build up London Bridge?
My fair lady.

Only God's Chief Cornerstone,
Cornerstone, Cornerstone,
Only God's Chief Cornerstone,
My fair lady.

ONE LITTLE SNOWFLAKE

One little snowflake,
   Looking like white lace,
Drifted from the sky
   With a sad, little face.

"I'm not very big
   To help water this whole earth;
How can a little snowflake
   Be of very much worth?"

Another little snowflake
   With a happy smile,
Floated down beside her friend
   And said, "We *are* worthwhile!"

"Many little snowflakes,
   Each one doing his own part,
Can together make a river,
   When we melt, heart-to-heart."

So each little girl and boy
   With smiles of love to give,
Can together make a river
   Bless the world in which we live.

IF TURNIP SEEDS GROW TURNIPS

If turnip seeds grow turnips,
　And greens grow spinach greens;
If carrot seeds grow carrots,
　And bean seeds bring up beans;
If lettuce seeds grow lettuce,
　And Brussel seeds grow sprouts;
If pea seeds always bring up peas —
　Then what goes in comes out!

So kind words bring up kindness,
　And bad words will grow sadness;
Forgiving words will grow forgiveness,
　Glad words will grow gladness!
So watch the little seeds you plant,
　In all you say and do;
For what you sow is what you reap!
　Be proud of what you grew!

WHAT'S THE NEWS
OF THE DAY?

What's the news of the day
  Good neighbor, I pray?
They say the King soon
  Will outshine the moon!

THE NOTHING-IMPOSSIBLE-POSSUM

Have you heard of the
  Nothing-Impossible-Possum,
Who dreamed of a flute
  Made of pink apple blossom?

And not just a flute
  That *one* possum could blow,
But a flute that would toot
  'Round the world in one go!

And not just a flute
  With one toot blown each day,
But a flute that would toot
  Morning, night in relay!

And not just a flute
  Blown at morning and night,
But a flute that would toot
  Every second in sight!

And not just a flute
  That each second would sound;
But a flute that would toot
  Every musical sound!

Low notes
And high notes,
And in-between shy notes;
And notes that would whistle and woo.
SING sounds,
And ZING sounds,
And echoing PING sounds,
And sounds ringing FOO-FEE-A-ROO!

Trill tunes
And hill tunes,
And happy-goodwill tunes;
And tunes to astound and amaze!
Whirled songs
And twirled songs,
And all-cross-the-world songs,
And songs everywhere in God's praise!

"It's really absurd,"
   Said a glum mockingbird,
"To be playing a flute night and day.
   Who would listen that long
   To a possum's flute song?
Take your dreams, sir, and throw them away."

"It's a possible dream,
   And I'll stay with my scheme,"
Said the Nothing-Impossible-Possum;
 "And a big flute brigade
   Will praise God in parade;
And I'll start with this pink apple blossom!"

So he carved out a flute
  That one possum could blow,
Then asked his good friend
  If he'd join on below.

His friend, the raccoon,
  Took a nice maple limb,
And soon shaped a flute
  To join onto the rim.

So sitting together
  They warbled a tune,
Which brought out a beaver
  Who knew the raccoon.

"I'm an expert with wood!
  If you fellows don't mind,
I'll join on my flute,
  Then we'll all play combined."

The three played together
  And woke up a rabbit,
Who said, "I'll be part
  Of this musical habit."

So now four were playing —
  The flute was quite long,
When up walked a duck
  Who joined in with the song.

"Come! Bring an extension,
  We've a long way to go,"
They all told the duck,
  So *he* joined on to blow!

They blew songs of praise
  With such sounds never heard,
That for miles through the forest
  They shocked every bird!

69

Soon everyone wanted
  To join on the flute;
With a piece here and there
  It stretched miles with each toot!

It went through the forest
  And over the hills,
With PING sounds and ZING sounds,
  And sounds full of trills.

Across the great mountains,
  And 'round river bends;
With each creature adding,
  The flute could not end!

It reached the North Pole,
  Where a big polar bear
Said, "I've enough breath
  To blow ten miles from here!"

So he lengthened the flute
   For ten miles 'cross the ice,
Where two penguins cried,
   "What a marvelous device!"

"Is this what is making
   Such music each day?
We'd like to join in
   And praise God, if we may."

"If God gave you breath,
   Then you're part of our throng,"
The polar bear smiled,
   "Come and join in our song."

Then down from the North Pole
  Came low notes and high;
The flute ever growing,
  With each passerby.

Creatures with long necks,
  And some with big snouts,
All happily blowing
  And praising with shouts!

Behold! Every second
  Of each night and day,
A round-the-world flute
  Toot-toot-tooted in play!

Low notes
And high notes,
And in-between shy notes;
And notes that would whistle and woo.
SING sounds,
And ZING sounds,
And echoing PING sounds,
And sounds ringing FOO-FEE-A-ROO!

Trill tunes
And hill tunes,
And happy-goodwill tunes;
And tunes to astound and amaze!
Whirled songs,
And twirled songs,
And all-cross-the-world songs,
And songs everywhere in God's praise!

And how did it start?
    With a pink apple blossom!
And the dream of that
    Nothing-Impossible-Possum!

SHALL WE GO A-SHARING?

"Old woman, old woman,
  Shall we go a-sharing?"
"Speak a little louder, sir,
  I'm very hard of hearing."
"Old woman, old woman,
  I love you very dearly."
"Thank you very kindly, sir,
  I hear you very clearly."

SNAIL, SNAIL

Snail, Snail,
Put out your horns,
Be glad! Be glad!
Don't be forlorn.
The trees clap hands,
The hills, they sing!
Don't you hear
The bluebells ring?
Come and join them!
Ring-a-ling!
God cares for us!
Come! Sing! Sing! Sing!

75

HEY, DIDDLE, DIDDLE

Hey, diddle, diddle,
  Me and my fiddle,
The cat sang along in tune;
  My little dog laughed
Enjoying our song,
  How God hung the stars and the moon!

LITTLE EARTHEN VESSELS

God has put a treasure
   In a little earthen pot.
It's such a precious treasure,
   Clean and pure, without a spot!

Yes! All across the world,
   Where the Name of Jesus sounds,
In little pots that love Him,
   This great treasure can be found,

IN...

Brown pots
And black pots,
And all-in-a-stack pots;
And pots that are fancy and plain;
In red pots
And white pots,
And heavy and light pots;
And yellow pots covered with cane.

In tall pots
And short pots,
And sturdy support-pots,
And tiny pots bobbing around;
In smooth pots
And rough pots,
And tumble-and-scuff pots,
And pots hidden way underground!

In clear pots
And flecked pots,
And close neck-to-neck pots,
And pots with a wee, little spout;
In north pots
And south pots,
And big open-mouth pots,
With handles on some; some without.

So that...

North, west, south and eastwards,
   And in any language, too,
You can ask God for this treasure
   To come in and live in you!

That's why all across the world,
   Boys and girls — and grown-ups, too,
Are the little earthen vessels
   For God's treasure to shine through.

DANDELION SEA SUMMER GAMES

Do you hear the music
  In Dandelion Sea?
It's time for Summer Games;
  Would you like to come with me?

There is such excitement,
  With bands and flags and noise!
It's a grand occasion
  For watching, girls and boys!

There's racing, flying, diving,
  And fun for everyone;
Look! They're giving medals.
  Listen! Let's see who won!

80

"Ladies and gentlemen,
Our judges agree
On these champions
At Dandelion Sea!"...

"The longest non-stop flight gold medal
Goes to Billy-Boy Blue Goose!
Sixteen hundred miles he flew —
Without a wing getting loose!"

199 FT.

200 FT.

"The champion of diving
Is Emperor Pat Penguin,
Who went down over two hundred feet —
A big gold medal to win!"

81

"The fastest bird we timed today
    Is the zooming, Spine-tailed Swift;
Over one hundred miles an hour!
    A gold medal for you, Swifty-Swift!"

"Boys and girls, let's stop to cheer
    The power of God, indeed,
Who makes His creatures fly and dive,
    Without a motor for speed!"

I WILL BLESS THE LORD AT ALL TIMES!...

PRAISE THE LORD!

OH, GIVE THANKS UNTO THE LORD!...

HIP HIP HOORAY!

"Well...
What is this group over here,
    Singing in the oak tree shade?
Hello, Bright-Bill! What's the meaning
    Of this Summer Games parade?"

"We're having a celebration,
    Though we didn't win medals today;
Stay and listen as we thank God
    For what we enjoy *every* day!"

Katy Kangaroo said…
    "I will thank Him for my pouch,
    Where all my babies ride and crouch!"

Mickey Monkey said…
    "I will thank Him for my tail,
    From which I hang, and swing and sail!"

Peter Pelican said…
    "I will thank Him for my sack,
    Where fishes for my lunch I pack!"

Tommy Turtle said...
  "I will thank Him for my shell,
  That makes a house that I love well!"

Mary Meadowlark said...
  "I will thank Him for my song,
  That makes you happy all day long!"

Sherry Sheep said...
  "I will thank Him for my fleece,
  That makes a boy's coat, piece by piece!"

"Boys and girls...
  The Bible says:
  'Let everything that has breath
  Praise the Lord!'

So...
  If penguins, pelicans, turtles, too,
  Can all be thankful —
  HOW ABOUT YOU!"

THERE WAS AN OLD WOMAN
LIVED UNDER A HILL

There was an old woman
    Lived under a hill.
She was an old woman
    Of very good will.

Baked apples she gave
    To children who came
To learn about Jesus,
    And call on His Name.

Great stories she told
    Of Samson and Paul,
And prophets of old
    Who answered God's call.

The children all loved her,
    For she was the one
Who told how God loved them,
    And sent His dear Son.

THE UPSIDE–DOWN
TOWN

Once upon a time,
  There was a strange, little town;
Where everything and everyone
  Was upside down!

The houses stood upon their roofs,
  And when you climbed in bed,
The stars outside were down below;
  Yet not a prayer was said!

A wooden sign outside the town
  Said, "TOPPLE Welcomes You!"
But if you tried to read it
  You would have to topple, too!

No visitors would ever come
  To do their shopping there;
For if they did, they would have to walk
  With their legs up in the air!

The boys and girls in Topple
  Didn't know they were upside down.
The ground to them was all sky-blue,
  And the sky was green and brown!

The great, wise King of Right-Side-Up
  Said, "I must send a man
To turn the upside-down town
  Right-side up, as I did plan.

The great, wise King had words of power
  To do such things, you see.
So he sent a man at chosen time
  In Topple's history.

This man brought words that shook the town,
  And turned it back from upside-down;
A few believed what this man said,
  And found themselves on feet, not head!

But others shut their eyes and ears,
  And cried, "This man just interferes!
He's upside-down, and not our town;
  We'll not obey his King or crown."

And so they stayed upon their heads,
   And when they climbed into their beds,
They hoped the next day's scenery
   Would be the same as usually.

The boys and girls, they listened well
   To all those words the King did tell;
And learned to pray at night in bed,
   And see the stars overhead.

So — still today in Topple town,
   Where many yet are upside-down,
It is the boys and girls who say,
   "Obey the King, and turn His way!"

TWO LITTLE DICKY BIRDS

Two little dicky birds
  Sitting on a wall;
One named Peter,
  The other named Paul.
"I'll pray," said Peter,
  "I'll pray," said Paul,
"Close eyes, Peter!"
  "Close eyes, Paul!"

AS TOMMY SNOOKS AND BESSY BROOKS

As Tommy Snooks and Bessy Brooks
  Were walking out one Sunday,
Said Tommy Snooks to Bessy Brooks,
  "Tomorrow will be Monday!"
Said Bessy Brooks to Tommy Snooks,
  "The next day will be Tuesday!"
Said Tommy Snooks to Bessy Brooks,
  "Let's call each day, 'Good News Day'!"

MATTHEW, MARK, LUKE AND JOHN

Matthew, Mark, Luke and John,
Wrote a Book that still lives on!
Not one word can pass away,
For these are words the Lord did say.

AS I WALKED BY MYSELF

As I walked by myself
And talked with myself,
Myself said unto me,
  "Look to the Lord,
  Pray to the Lord,
  For the Lord, He cares for thee."

I answered myself,
And said to myself,
"I will take your advice and agree;
  I'll look to you, Lord,
  And pray to you, Lord;
  Thank you for loving me."

SOLOMON GRUNDY

Solomon Grundy said one Sunday,
 "I think that I can make a Monday.
I will improve the present day
    And add two extra hours for play."

"Not only that, the sun will shine
    From four-o'clock to half-past nine.
I'll make it rain at my command,
    On chosen ones across the land."

So Solomon woke at half-past three,
    Ran up the hill and climbed a tree.
And as the time was nearing four,
    Solomon Grundy gave a roar!

"Come up, _now_, sun! Begin my day!
    Come two hours early for extra play."
But no light came — to his surprise!
    Shout as he would, the sun didn't rise!

"The sun can't hear me; it's out of sight;
    Those extra hours I'll make tonight."
Then as he jumped down from the tree,
    An owl that watched on said, "That can't be!"

"The sunrise and sunset you can't persuade,
    For this is the day the Lord hath made."
But Solomon Grundy, haughtily,
    Said, "This is the day named after me!"

"It's Grunday today, I'll make it rain
  Down on the fields of Farmer Slade's grain.
He is deserving; honest and fair;
  I'll tell a big cloud to rain over there."

He looked all around; no cloud was in sight.
  "I'll push one together with all my might.
There must be a way to make clouds," said he,
  Then a fawn that watched on said, "That can't be!"

"God gives the rain for *all*, not just Slade,
  For this is the day the Lord hath made!"
But Solomon Grundy, haughtily,
  Said, "This is the day named after me!"

Solomon sighed, "My day I can't waste,
  Those two extra hours I must find in haste.
It's now two-o'clock! I'll jump on this stack,
  And insist the sun go two hours back!"

"Sun, *please* go back at the hour's chime!"
  But the sun stayed in place in perfect time.
"There must be a way to make time," said he;
  Then a dove that watched on said, "That can't be!"

"God has fixed time, you cannot evade,
  For this is the day the Lord hath made!"
But Solomon Grundy, wearily,
  Said, "This day I tried to name after me!"

95

"But I can't make a day, I can't make it rain,
   I can't guide the sun, it's hard to explain.
I can't find the time or master-key,
   To make up a day named after me."

So Solomon Grundy began to see
   That GOD makes the days, and so said he,
"I'll stop this foolish, day-making crusade,
   And rejoice in the day the LORD hath made!"

BENJAMIN BUMBLEBEE
AND THE GIANT TUMBLEWEED

Nestled in a sunflower
  In Dandelion Sea,
Reading his daily lesson,
  Was Benjamin Bumblebee.

The sunflower began to sway,
  As a breeze began to blow;
But Benjamin kept on reading,
  And rocking to and fro.

"If I say this verse ten times,
  Then perhaps I'll come to see
What these words can really mean
  To a learning bumblebee!"

"All things work together for good
  To those who love the Lord;
All things work together for good
  To those who love the Lord."

"All things work together for good—
   Now, is that three times or four?
All things work together…" "SWOOSH",
   In rushed a wind with a roar!

It blew the roofs off houses,
   And lifted a hive of bees;
Then took Charlie Cricket's mail bag
   Sailing over the trees!

ZOOM! went Grandpa Mole's balloon;
   SWISH! went thousands of seeds!
And then that mighty wind swept up
   A giant tumbleweed!

It raced this way and that way,
   And went bouncing everywhere;
Then bumped the flower with Benjamin
   And took him riding in the air!

98

Up above the tree-tops,
  Caught in the crackling wood,
Benjamin kept shouting,
  "All things work together for good!"

"Be brave, my friend, all's well!"
  Shouted dear old Grandpa Mole;
Then whispered to himself,
  "Hmmm…but *I'm* safe in this hole!"

"It's easy cheering down there,"
  Benjamin gave a shout;
"It's hard to see that all is well
  Up here in this roundabout!"

"WOO-AH!" — the big wind roared again,
  And Benjamin flew higher,
Soaring past Grandpa Mole's balloon
  In his tumbleweed high-flyer!

99

Then snap, crack, crunch and whirling,
  The tumbleweed plunged down
On Mrs. Mouse's small green lawn,
  At the other side of town.

The lawn was filled with leaves
  That the wind had blown in there;
Mrs. Mouse was squeaking,
  "This is more than I can bear."

But quickly snatching, catching,
  Benjamin rolled around,
Gathering leaves on every point,
  'Til not one was left on the ground!

Then off again on the gusty wind,
  In his giant tumbleweed,
Benjamin rode as the captain
  Of his trusty, clean-up steed.

MRS. MOUSE

Rolling, blowing through the clouds,
  And turning end on end,
Benjamin heard Mrs. Mouse
  Calling, "Thank you, friend!"

"Well, that's one deed I helped with
  That sheds light upon this verse,
'All things work together for good...'
  Even when things seem worse!"

"Oh, what is this that's flying
  Like a yellow-handled sail?
I do believe it must be
  Charlie Cricket's own air mail!"

"My tumbleweed can save it
  With a crackly, wooden snag."
And reaching very quickly,
  Benjamin caught the lost mail bag.

HUFF! PUFF! A cloud blew round him,
  And he couldn't see at all
Where the wind was blowing him.
  He felt so lost and small.

He didn't see the mail bag
  Fall down from the tumbleweed,
And drop at Charlie Cricket's feet
  As fast as air-mail speed.

"Thank you, thank you," Charlie cried,
  "You're the hero of the day.
The letters are all saved,
  When I thought they'd blown away!"

"A hero, really, am I?
  While I'm tossed and blown about?
I cannot understand this,
  And that's without a doubt!"

"Well...I'll think of something hopeful
    While I'm in this fluffy cloud;
I know! I'll say my verse again,
    And shout it very loud!"

"All things work together for good
    To those who love the Lord;
All things work together for good
    To those who love the Lord!"

He shouted to the big wind,
    "I will safely land — and soon!"
When all at once he felt
    The ropes of Grandpa Mole's balloon.

He hung on tightly to one end,
    As the cloud was blown away;
Then suddenly — the wind was still;
    He began to gently sway.

103

Softly, softly, he floated down;
   Such a funny sight was he,
Inside a tumbleweed balloon
   Over Dandelion Sea.

Grandpa Mole was cheering him
   For saving his balloon;
While Lucy Ladybug
   Played him a "Happy Landing" tune.

"Dear Benjamin! You've landed!
   What adventures you've withstood;
And I heard you shouting in the air,
   'All things work together for good!'"

104

"Yes, dear Grandpa Mole, that's true,
  But before I blew away,
I didn't know those words would fit
  The things that happened today."

"It's hard for just a bumblebee
  To learn in one short day,
But I believe these words are true,
  And I'll understand someday, how:

  'All things work
  Together for good
  To those who
  Love the Lord!'"

BECAUSE JESUS LIVES

Little seeds can grow like this,
Because Jesus lives!

Little eggs can hatch a chick,
Because Jesus lives!

The sun can shine upon my face,
Because Jesus lives!

A bird can find its way through space,
Because Jesus lives!

I can feel the ocean's spray,
Because Jesus lives!

God will hear me when I pray,
Because Jesus lives!

I can pick the golden rod,
Because Jesus lives!

I can go to live with God,
Because Jesus lives!

STAR LIGHT, STAR BRIGHT

Star light, star bright,
  Guide us on our way tonight;
I wish I may, I wish I might,
  See the King this very night.

NOW I LAY ME DOWN TO SLEEP

Now I lay me down to sleep,
  I pray the Lord my soul to keep;
I know He watches over me,
  So I can sleep as safe can be!

CONTENTS

" Let Everything
That Hath Breath
Praise The Lord!"

"... A Little Child Shall Lead Them."

ABOUT THE AUTHOR . . .

Best-Seller author, Marjorie Ainsborough Decker, is originally from Liverpool, England. As author, playwright and well-loved speaker, she has an extensive ministry in the U.S.A. and overseas.

Marjorie is a recognized student of the Word. She brings fresh enthusiasm and dynamic faith to biblical scholarship. Her reputation as a popular Bible teacher has earned many invitations as a featured speaker at seminars, banquets and convocations. Genuinely committed to the Gospel of The Lord Jesus Christ, Mrs. Decker brings the love of God and His message to every age and situation. She speaks with authority and credits God with giving her something to share.

An inspiring dimension to this gifted author is her encouraging role as a mother. She and her husband, Dale, have raised four athletic sons, Glen, Bradley, Kevin and Keith, two of which have graduated from Wheaton College. Marjorie is a sports fan who believes Christ can shine in the thick of competition and is warmly received by many athletes. The family resides in Western Colorado.

Marjorie is also the major illustrator of THE CHRISTIAN MOTHER GOOSE TREASURY. From a background of tremendous talents and interests, stems her ability to blend allegorical insights with colorful depiction.

Another facet of the "Christian Mother Goose" ministry is the full-scale musical production, *A DAY AT DANDELION SEA*. Written and directed by Mrs. Decker, the play is packed with wit, charm and penetrating biblical insight. Having been premiered as a stage production, it is now underway as a television special. It is a fitting fulfillment of the desires of a little girl in England who sang and danced in the street to bring courage to the war-laden hearts of those around her.

After World War II, Marjorie came to the United States as a young bride, where she discovered the challenges of building a life and home in the Rocky Mountains, suffering the death of her first husband, even operating a bulldozer to plow her way out of a snow storm.

This engaging author has used her ready wit and imagination to produce the "Christian Mother Goose Series" -- a landmark contribution to the world of classical Christian literature. Her original work, THE CHRISTIAN MOTHER GOOSE BOOK, has established her as a Best-Selling Christian storyteller.

Marjorie Ainsborough Decker's life is a storybook testimony of adventures in creative Christian living. She has touched the lives of the young, inspired the lives of the elderly, and has now given us a new dimension of historical allegory in THE CHRISTIAN MOTHER GOOSE TRILOGY. THE CHRISTIAN MOTHER GOOSE TREASURY is Part II of this *lifetime classic collection.*

Contributing illustrator, Glenna Fae Hammond, has brought some of the Dandelion Sea characters to life in her work found in THE TREASURY. Mrs. Hammond is a free-lance artist. She and her husband, Tom, are the parents of three children, Ronnie, Cindy and Bobby. The family lives in Eastern Colorado.

Marjorie Ainsborough Decker